THE
FOLLETT
BEGINNING-TO-READ
SERIES

Have You Seen My Brother?

BY ELIZABETH GUILFOILE

illustrated by Mary Stevens

Follett Publishing Company

Chicago

Library of Congress Catalog Card Number: 62-15668

SBN 695-43685-6 Titan binding   SBN 695-83685-4 Trade binding   Eighth Printing

Andrew asked the milkman,
"Have you seen my brother?
He has red hair."

5

The milkman put the milk on the steps.

"No, I haven't seen a boy with red hair."

Andrew asked the mailman,

"Have you seen my brother?

He has red hair.

He has freckles."

The mailman put the mail in the box.

"No, I haven't seen a boy

with red hair and freckles."

Andrew asked the truck driver,
"Have you seen my brother?
He has red hair and freckles.
He wears blue jeans."

The truck driver got on the truck.

"No," he said.

"I haven't seen him."

Andrew asked the man at the gas station,

"Have you seen my brother?

He has red hair and freckles.

He wears blue jeans."

"No," said the man.

"No, I haven't seen him."

Andrew asked the bus driver,

"Have you seen my brother?

He has red hair and freckles.

He wears blue jeans."

"No," said the bus driver.

"No, I haven't seen a boy with red hair."

14

Andrew asked the grocer,

"Have you seen my brother?

He has red hair, freckles, and blue jeans."

"No," said the grocer.

"Where did you lose him?"

Andrew said,

"I lost him downtown.

We came downtown together."

The grocer weighed the apples.

He said, "Ask the policeman.

He finds lost boys."

Andrew asked a woman,

"Have you seen the policeman?

I lost my brother.

I lost him downtown.

The policeman will help me find him."

The woman said,

"There is the policeman.

The policeman is on the corner."

Andrew said to the policeman,

"Mr. Policeman, my brother is lost.

Can you help me find him?"

21

The policeman said,

"Let's go to the police station.

Policemen take lost boys to the

police station."

The policeman and Andrew went
to the police station.

Andrew said,

"There he is!

There is my brother.

There is Bobby."

Bobby had red hair.

He had freckles.

He wore blue jeans.

Bobby said,

"Andrew, where have you been?

I looked for you everywhere."

Andrew said,

"I was looking for you.

I asked everyone.

Then the policeman told me where

to find lost boys."

Then Andrew said,

"Thank you, Mr. Policeman.

Thank you for finding my brother.

Bobby, let's go home."

HAVE YOU SEEN MY BROTHER?

Reading Level: Level One. *Have You Seen My Brother?* has a total vocabulary of 83 words. It has been tested in first grade classes, where it was read with ease.

Uses of This Book: Reading for fun and in connection with primary social studies. Andrew loses his brother and seeks help from the bus driver, milkman, mailman, and other community workers. Children will enjoy the surprise ending.

Word List

All of the 83 words used in *Have You Seen My Brother?* are listed. Regular plurals (*-s*) and regular verb forms (*-s, -ed, -ing*) of words already on the list are not listed separately, but the endings are given in parentheses after the word.

5	Andrew	red			a
	ask (ed)	hair			boy (s)
	the				with
	milkman				
	have	**6**	put		
	you		milk	**7**	mailman
	seen		on		freckles
	my		steps		
	brother		no		
	he		I	**8**	mail
	has		haven't		in

box
and

9 truck
driver
wears
blue
jeans

10 got
said
him

11 man
at
gas
station

13 bus

15 grocer

16 where
did

lose

17 lost
downtown
we
came
together

18 weighed
apples
policeman
finds

19 woman
will
help
me
find (ing)

20 there
is
corner

21 Mr.
can

22 let's
go
to

police
policemen
take

24 Bobby

25 had

26 been
look (ed) (ing)

for
everywhere

27 was
everyone
then
told

28 thank
home

The Follett BEGINNING-TO-READ Books

Purpose of the Beginning-to-Read Books: To provide easy-to-read materials that will appeal to the interests of primary children. Careful attention is given to vocabulary load and sentence length, but the first criterion is interest to children.

Reading Levels: These books are written at three reading levels, indicated by one, two, or three dots beneath the *Beginning-to-Read* symbol on the back cover. *Level One* books can be read by first grade children in the last half of the school year. As children increase their reading ability they will be able to enjoy *Level Two* books. And as they grow further in their reading ability they will progress to *Level Three* books. Some first grade children will read *Level Two* and *Level Three* books. Many third graders, and even some fourth graders, will read and enjoy *Level One* and *Level Two* books, as well as *Level Three* books. The range of interest of *Beginning-to-Read* books stretches far beyond their reading level.

Use of the Beginning-to-Read Books: Because of their high interest and readability, these books are ideal for independent reading by primary children—at school, in the library, and at home. The books may also be incorporated into the basic reading program to develop children's interests, expand their vocabularies, and improve word-attack skills. It has been suggested that they might serve as the foundation for a skillfully directed reading program. Many *Beginning-to-Read* books correlate with the social studies, science, and other subject fields. All will help children grow in the language arts. Children will read the *Beginning-to-Read* books with confidence, with success, and with real enjoyment.